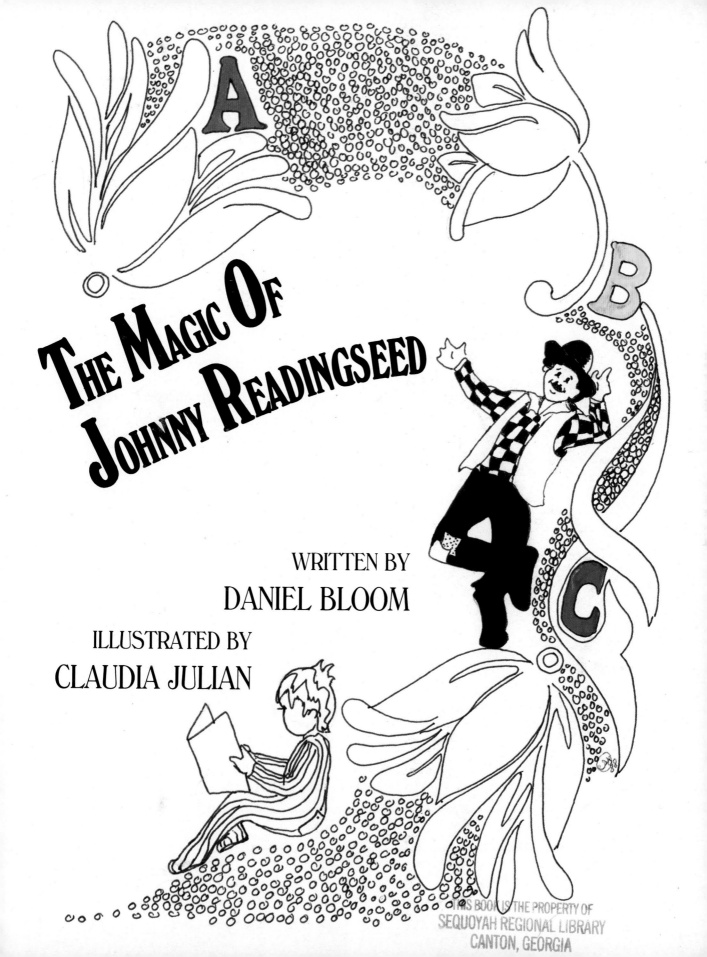

The Magic Of Johnny Readingseed

WRITTEN BY
DANIEL BLOOM

ILLUSTRATED BY
CLAUDIA JULIAN

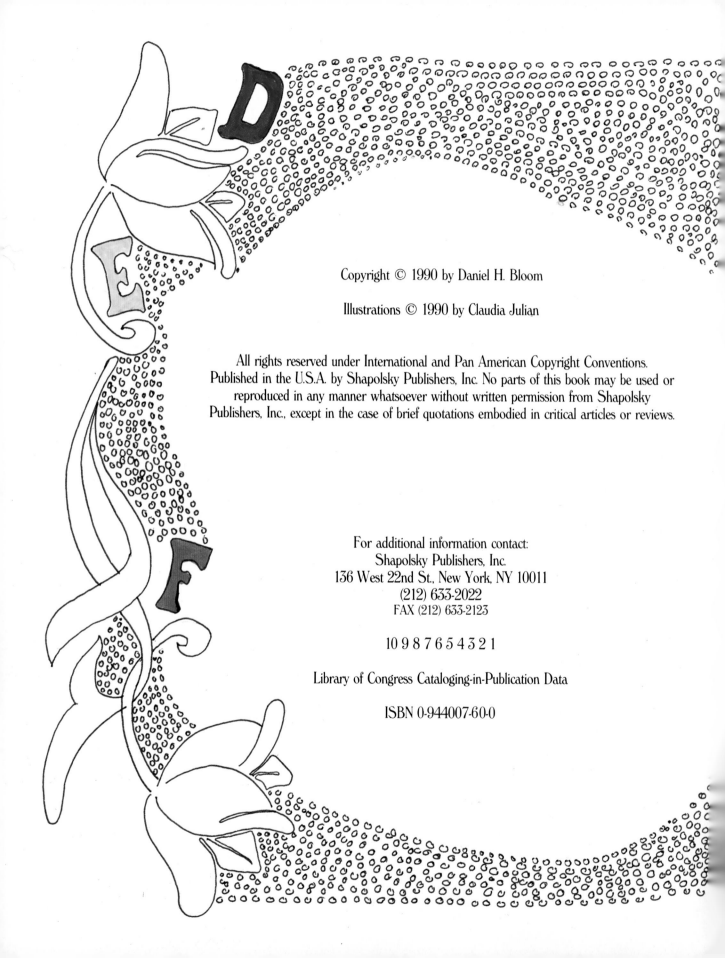

For additional information contact:
Shapolsky Publishers, Inc.
136 West 22nd St., New York, NY 10011
(212) 633-2022
FAX (212) 633-2123

10 9 8 7 6 5 4 3 2 1

Library of Congress Cataloging-in-Publication Data

ISBN 0-944007-60-0

Far, Far Away,

in the land of ABC,
there lives a very magical fellow named
Johnny Readingseed. He lives in a
magical house with a magical cat and
a magical dog and in his home you
can find every book
that was ever written...

ONCE UPON A TIME.....

When Johnny Readingseed
was a little boy, he learned to read
because reading was fun. Whenever he
opened up a new book, he was
always excited because he
knew that the words
would take him on
adventures into far
away worlds and he knew that
every time he turned the page a
new picture or thought would be
awaiting him!

Now, dear children, right from the start, I must tell you that Johnny Readingseed was not an ordinary man. No, Johnny Readingseed had magical powers that allowed him to fly in the air.

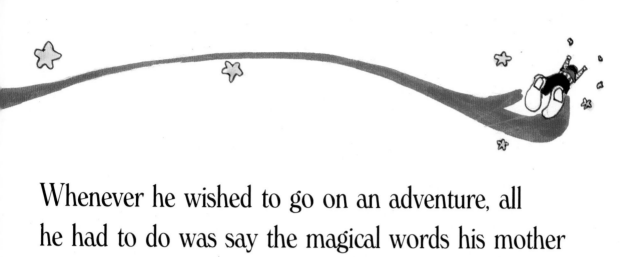

Whenever he wished to go on an adventure, all
he had to do was say the magical words his mother
had taught him "ABCDiery, EFGdiary, XYZomerry!"
and—poof!—off he would go, flying this
way and that, upside down
and sideways, wherever
he wished to go.

When Johnny Readingseed grew up into a grown-up sort of man he decided that since he liked reading so much he would spend his time flying around the world and teaching children about the joys of reading. He decided, in a very magical way, to become the world's Ambassador of Reading and to visit children in every land wherever books were read. Maybe that is why his mother and father had named him Johnny Readingseed when he was born, so that he could spread the seeds of reading into every school and home...

Sometimes Johnny Readingseed comes to visit children when they are lying in bed reading their favorite book. Sometimes he comes to visit children when they are sleeping and he appears in their dreams. And sometimes, just sometimes, Johnny Readingseed comes to visit children in their classrooms, if the teacher says it is okay.

Let me tell you about the time Johnny Readingseed came to visit me...

I was about 5 years old, more like 5 and a half or five and three quarters, something like that, and I was just learning to read. Dinner was over at my house and I was getting ready for bed.

Downstairs my parents were watching television, but after I put on my pajamas, I crawled into bed with a shiny new book I had received on my birthday.

It was a book with words and pictures, just like this one, and I was very excited about reading it.

Do you ever like to read underneath your covers with a flashlight? That's what I like to do sometimes. And on the night that Johnny Readingseed came to my house, that's exactly what I was doing!

Well, no sooner had I opened up the book and turned to the first page...when all of a sudden, in a brilliant flash of light, a little man popped out of my book, a magical, funny kind of man with a small black hat and rib-tickling laugh. Whenever he laughed, my ribs tickled!

"Who are you?" I asked, pointing my flashlight at him.

"I am Johnny Readingseed," the magical little man answered. "Do you know your ABC's?"

"Of course, I know my ABC's," I replied. "Everybody knows their ABC's."

"Show me then!" responded Johnny Readingseed, who, when I looked real hard at him, reminded me alot of my Uncle Eddie, but I knew it couldn't be Uncle Eddie because he lived so far away from my house. I recited the whole alphabet:

DEFGHIJKLMNOPQRSTUVWXYZ

"Very good!" replied Johnny Readingseed, tipping his hat in my direction. "Splendid! Now I shall tell you a secret."

"A secret?" I asked, whispering beneath the covers so my parents wouldn't hear us talking. "A secret about what?"

"It's a secret about a secret," whispered Johnny Readingseed back to me. "And this is what the secret is: if you can learn to read a book all by yourself, then you will always have magic in your life!"

"What's magic?" I had to ask, not sure if I understood what magic was.

"Magic is when you have a dream and fly from house to house. Magic is when you open a book and the whole world opens up before you. Magic is when

somebody magical like me comes to visit you when you're reading." I loved listening to Johnny Readingseed talk.

His voice was so...

...so magical!

"You mean all that is happening to me right now is part of the magic?" I asked.

"Precisely," replied Johnny Readingseed.

"Could you, uh, er, teach me how to fly, sir?" I asked.

"Oh yes, I could teach you lots of things, lots of things, but first you must learn to read!"

"I will try my best," I replied. "I'm learning right now, even!"

"Good, good!" replied Johnny Readingseed, who by now had slipped out from beneath the covers and was flying all over the room. I could hardly believe my eyes! This was an adventure I would never forget.

In the morning, I told myself, I would tell my teacher at school all about Johnny Readingseed and his magical, magical visit to my house...

But as I was trying to ask Johnny Readingseed another question, my eyes began to get heavier and heavier and I was getting sleepier and sleepier.

"Johnny Readingseed," I called out, "I am getting tired. Will you come back again tomorrow night and take me on another adventure?"

"Tomorrow night, I must visit the homes of other boys and girls for there are many children who are looking for me," replied Johnny Readingseed. "But I will come back to visit you someday soon."

My eyes were getting really sleepy by now and I was trying very hard to stay awake. I didn't want to fall

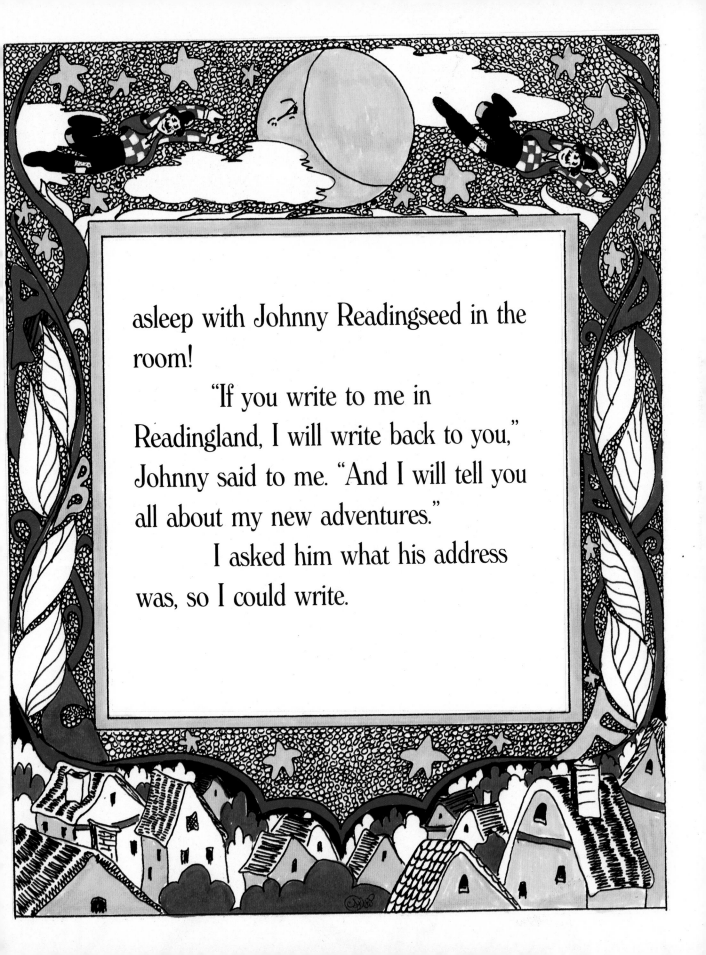

asleep with Johnny Readingseed in the room!

"If you write to me in Readingland, I will write back to you," Johnny said to me. "And I will tell you all about my new adventures."

I asked him what his address was, so I could write.

"You can write to me," replied Johnny Readingseed,
at this address:

Johnny Readingseed

Post Office Box 555

Auke Bay, Alaska

99821

and if you need help addressing your envelope to me and
putting on a stamp, ask your mother or father, or if you're at
school, ask your teacher.

By this time, I was in the middle of a beautiful dream and in the dream I found myself in a place called Readingland. There I could see Johnny Readingseed's very own magical house with his magical cat and his magical dog and when I opened the door I saw Johnny Readingseed himself inside the house reading all the children's letters from all over the world. I knew then that this was indeed a dream come true and I am happy that there is a Johnny Readingseed in the world.

And I <u>do</u> love reading.

And I love Johnny Readingseed, too. He is very special...

And you know, reading <u>is</u> fun!

THE END